Katie Van Camp

Harry and Horsie

Illustrated by
Lincoln Agnew

JE
Van
c.6

Central Rappahannock Regional Library
1201 Caroline Street
Fredericksburg, VA 22401

Balzer & Bray
An Imprint of HarperCollinsPublishers

To the real Harry (and his Horsie) with love

A Note from Harry's Dad

Hello, kids, and get ready for an amazing bedtime adventure. It's a story about the surprising things that can happen with bubbles. Now I know there's nothing more fun than blowing giant, beautiful bubbles. They glide and float and hop and sometimes pop on your head, but you can never be quite sure where they are going or even how far they might travel. You're about to hear the story of my son, Harry, and his best pal, Horsie, and the night that . . . well, I'll let you find out for yourself. But the next time you're blowing bubbles, keep a close eye on them. You could be headed for a magical journey of your own.

—Dave Letterman

Harry and Horsie
Text copyright © 2009 by Katie Van Camp
Illustrations copyright © 2009 by Lincoln Agnew

Manufactured in China.
All rights reserved. No part of this book may be used or reproduced in any manner whatsoever without written permission except in the case of brief quotations embodied in critical articles and reviews. For information address HarperCollins Children's Books, a division of HarperCollins Publishers, 10 East 53rd Street, New York, NY 10022. www.harpercollinschildrens.com
Library of Congress Cataloging-in-Publication Data is available.
ISBN 978-0-06-175598-9 (trade bdg.)

Typography by Dana Fritts
09 10 11 12 13 SCP 10 9 8 7 6 5 4 3 2 1 ❖ First Edition

It was way past bedtime, but Harry wasn't tired. Neither was Horsie.

The moon was keeping them awake. It was shining on the shelf where Harry's brand-new Super Duper Bubble Blooper had been put away for the night.

"Come on," Harry whispered.

Wherever Harry went, Horsie went too, so they crept across the room.

Harry knew exactly how to get his Bubble Blooper down.

And, of course, Horsie helped him.

They bounced off the ceiling
and bumped into the walls.

Then a bubble picked up
Harry's train and . . .

Harry laughed as he chased the bubbles.

More of them scooped up his cars and his planes and his shoes.

BLOOP went his books and *BLOOP* went his whirligigs.

And then, all of a sudden, a giant bubble *BLOOPED* and swept up . . .

And it carried him up and away.

There was no time to lose!
Harry put on his helmet and
grabbed his goggles.

Then he jumped aboard his
rocket ship . . . and took off to
find his friend.
  Harry blasted past Venus and
did a loop around Mars.
  But there was no sign of Horsie.

Harry didn't find Horsie on Saturn either, but he did find his cars. They were racing around Saturn's rings, tearing toward the finish line.

"Go, Red!" Harry cheered.

Then he took off for the Milky Way.

When he arrived, he saw something moving among the stars.

But it wasn't Horsie—it was Kitty. She was having a lovely time in space, with milk drops on her whiskers and stardust on her face.

"Have you seen Horsie?" Harry asked.

Kitty shook her head and mewed.

Harry was really starting to worry. He missed Horsie.

Then in the distance Harry saw something on the edge of the crescent moon. He looked closer.

Could it be?

"Hold on, I'm coming!"

Fast! Super fast! *WAY TOO FAST!*

Harry steered clear of a comet and swooped around a satellite.

When at last he arrived, Harry jumped onto
the moon and slid down to rescue his friend.
Harry was very happy to see Horsie.
And Horsie was happy to see Harry too.

"Let's head home now," Harry said,
hugging Horsie tight.
"Next time we go on an adventure,
let's go together, okay?"
Horsie liked that idea.

Because wherever Harry went, Horsie went too.